W9-ACT-559

The Trouble with Tilly Trumble

by
Lynn Manuel

illustrations by
Diane Greenseid

Harry N. Abrams, Inc., Publishers

The art in this book was created using acrylic paint on illustration board.

A portion of the illustrator's royalties for this book will be donated
to People for the Ethical Treatment of Animals (PETA).

Production Manager: Jonathan Lopes

Library of Congress Cataloging-in-Publication Data:

Manuel, Lynn.
The trouble with Tilly Trumble / by Lynn Manuel ; illustrated by Diane Greenseid.
p. cm.
Summary: A collector of broken-down old chairs that are on their last
legs, Tilly Trumble finally finds the perfect "four-legged, scruffy old
thing" to fill the empty space in front of the fireplace.
ISBN 0-8109-5972-0
[1. Chairs—Fiction. 2. Dogs—Fiction.] I. Greenseid, Diane, ill. II. Title.

PZ7.M3192Tro 2006
[E]—dc22
2005015468

Printed and bound in China
10 9 8 7 6 5 4 3 2 1

Harry N. Abrams, Inc.
115 West 18th Street
New York, NY 10011
www.abramsbooks.com

Abrams is a subsidiary of
LA MARTINIÈRE
GROUPE

In a house at the end of Potato-Peel Lane, there lived an old woman who loved chairs.

Tilly Trumble never had more than a few pennies to rub together, but every week she put on her fancy hat and her sturdy shoes, and off she went to make the rounds of the yard sales, flea markets, and swap meets, looking for old chairs that other folks were chucking out.

She brought home broken-down old chairs that were on their last legs.

Lumpy, flowered, plump old chairs
that sagged and dipped.

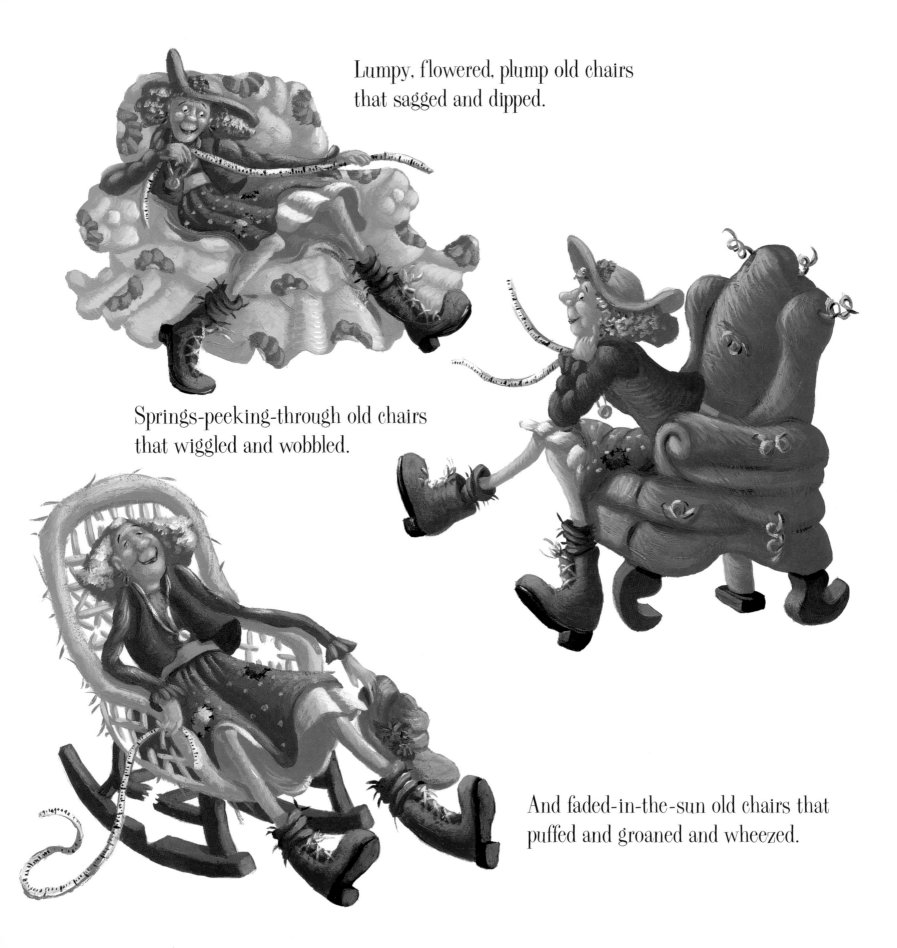

Springs-peeking-through old chairs
that wiggled and wobbled.

And faded-in-the-sun old chairs that
puffed and groaned and wheezed.

Down the lane Tilly would come, pulling an old chair behind her, with all the neighbors rolling their eyes and shaking their heads as she went by.

"Now, Tilly Trumble!" they would say. "What do you want with another four-legged, scruffy old thing like that?"

But Tilly never gave a fig what they had to say.

Tilly thought she was very lucky to live in a house spilling over with chairs—all of them holding out their arms, inviting her to cozy up in their laps.

But sometimes, when she was sitting in the old chair with the tassled cushions that didn't match, she would stare at the empty spot by the fire, the only spot in the whole house that was bare. Tilly could never find just the right chair to fill that empty place.

There were times when she thought a moth-eaten old chair with cinnamon-colored polka dots would do nicely. And other times when she thought a scratched-up old rocking chair with a cracked back might be better. But no, it couldn't be just any old thing. It had to be a four-legged, scruffy old thing that was really something else!

And then one day, when Tilly came home from a chucking-out sale, she found an unexpected visitor on her front porch, plunked down in one of her stuffing-poking-out old chairs. And Tilly didn't like it. Not one bit!

"I see you've made yourself quite comfortable," she said.

And that plunked-down, scruffy old dog just gave his tail a little wag as if to say he was quite comfy indeed, thank you very much!

"Scoot!" said Tilly, and then, "Scat!"

But that scruffy old dog did not scoot. And that scruffy old dog did not scat. So Tilly went into the house and she gave the door a slam!

But that night, just as Tilly was drifting off to sleep, she heard wind whistling in the eaves, and she found herself wondering if that dog was shivery. And the more she wondered about it, the more she tossed and turned, until finally she got out of bed and let that scruffy old dog come in out of the cold.

"Just for tonight!" she said, wagging a finger at him.

The next morning, as soon as Tilly was up and about, that scruffy old dog went out and fetched the newspaper from behind the raspberry bushes.

"You stop that right now!" said Tilly. "Do not try to butter me up!"

And without another word, she marched into the kitchen
and made breakfast—with too many sausages.

When that dog had finished every last one, Tilly opened the door
and flapped her arms up and down. "Shoo!" she said. "You cannot
stay here! I do not want a pet!"

But as Tilly stood there flapping, the scruffy old dog sat down
and put out his paw to shake hands.

"How funny you are!" said Tilly.

She gave the matter some thought and decided that perhaps he could stay until suppertime. Then, of course, he would have to be on his way.

But when suppertime came, the creaky old kitchen chair— the one with the oops-a-daisy stains all over it—held out its arms and invited that dog to sit in its lap. And when he did, Tilly had no choice but to add more meat to her stew.

After supper, Tilly put on her fancy hat and her sturdy shoes, and off she went to tack up posters around the neighborhood asking the owner of a scruffy old dog to come and fetch him— lickety split! That dog, of course, went right along with her.

"Now, that's really something!" said one of the neighbors.

"That's something else!" said another neighbor.

The weeks went by and nobody came to fetch that scruffy old dog. In time, Tilly got used to his company. Sometimes they made the rounds of the yard sales, flea markets, and swap meets together looking for just the right chair for that spot by the fire. Sometimes they sat outside in the old porch chairs, and Tilly showed that dog her scrapbook filled with tufts of stuffing and bits of fabric from old chairs that used to be and weren't anymore. And sometimes they just sat and watched the stars come out.

Every now and again, Tilly would look at that scruffy old dog and say, "I shan't give you a name. No point to it, you know. It's just a matter of time before I send you on your way."

And then one Sunday that dog went out to fetch the paper. He was gone before Tilly could stop him. And that was a shame because the paper wasn't delivered on Sundays.

All morning Tilly waited for him to come back. First she waited by the front window in the old winged chair, the one with the buttons hanging down from loops.

Then she sat on the porch in the threadbare, satiny old chair with the zigzaggy splits in it, and waited some more.

And then, for the longest time, she waited by the front gate in the propped-up old wooden chair with the missing leg.

Finally, she put on her fancy hat and her sturdy shoes and she set off to find that scruffy old dog.

She walked up one street and down another. She looked this way and that.

When she passed a yard sale, a lady wearing jangly earrings called out, "Would you be interested in a moth-eaten old chair with cinnamon-colored polka dots?"

"No thanks," said Tilly. "I'm looking for something else."

At a flea market on the corner, a man with a cane said, "I can give you a good deal on a scratched-up old rocking chair with a cracked back."

"No thanks," said Tilly. "I'm looking for something else."

But that scruffy old dog was nowhere to be seen.

When it got very late, Tilly turned around and started home.

"I don't mind," she told herself. "That scruffy old dog has long overstayed his welcome. And now I shall have plenty of stew left over for tomorrow!"

When Tilly opened her front gate, she stopped and blinked in surprise. There by the door was that scruffy old dog! And beside him was a newspaper—a long-forgotten newspaper tossed under somebody's shrubs ages ago. And Tilly knew that scruffy old dog must have searched all day to find it.

As he put out his paw to shake hands, Tilly held out her arms instead. And when he jumped into her lap, she hugged him and hugged him and hugged him!

"You really are something else!" she said. "And Something Else is just what I shall call you!"

When Tilly opened her front gate, she stopped and blinked in surprise. There by the door was that scruffy old dog! And beside him was a newspaper—a long-forgotten newspaper tossed under somebody's shrubs ages ago. And Tilly knew that scruffy old dog must have searched all day to find it.

As he put out his paw to shake hands, Tilly held out her arms instead. And when he jumped into her lap, she hugged him and hugged him and hugged him!

"You really are something else!" she said. "And Something Else is just what I shall call you!"

She realized, right then and there, that she had found just the right four-legged, scruffy old thing to fill that empty spot by the fire.

And now, in a house at the end of Potato-Peel Lane, there lives an old woman who loves chairs . . . almost as much as she loves Something Else!